P9-DGZ-507

🐝 little bee books

An imprint of Bonnier Publishing USA
251 Park Avenue South, New York, NY 10010
Copyright © 2018 by Bonnier Publishing USA

Library of Congress Cataloging-in-Publication Data
Names: Newton, A. I., author.
Title: The mystery valentine / by A. I. Newton; illustrated by Anjan Sarkar.
Description: First edition. | New York, NY: Little Bee, [2018] | Series: The
alien next door; book 5 | Summary: Harris and Roxy try to help Zeke the
alien over his confusion about Valentine's Day, and to figure out who sent
him an anonymous candy-gram. | Identifiers: LCCN 2018030540 (print)
Subjects: | CYAC: Extraterrestrial beings—Fiction. | Valentine's Day—Fiction. |
Schools—Fiction. | Friendship—Fiction. | Science Fiction. | BISAC: JUVENILE
FICTION / Readers / Chapter Books. | JUVENILE FICTION / Science Fiction. |
JUVENILE FICTION / Holidays & Celebrations / Valentine's Day.
Classification: LCC PZ7.1.N498 (ebook) | LCC PZ7.1.N498 Mys 2018 (print)
DDC [Fic]—dc23 | LC record available at https://lccn.loc.gov/2018030540

Printed in the United States of America LAK 1118
ISBN 978-1-4998-0726-4 (hardcover)
First Edition 10 9 8 7 6 5 4 3 2 1
ISBN 978-1-4998-0725-7 (paperback)
First Edition 10 9 8 7 6 5 4 3 2 1
ISBN 978-1-4998-0727-1 (ebook)

littlebeebooks.com
bonnierpublishingusa.com

THE ALIEN NEXT DOOR

THE MYSTERY VALENTINE

by A. I. Newton
illustrated by Anjan Sarkar

little bee books

TABLE OF CONTENTS

ZEKE WALKED INTO JEFFERSON Elementary School. Since his arrival on Earth from the planet Tragas a few months ago, he began to feel more and more comfortable with Earth customs every day. At first, everything on this new planet seemed strange to him.

Now, even something that was
scary at first, like walking into school,
was no big deal.

Except for today.

When Zeke entered the building this February morning, he was shocked by what he saw. The walls were covered with bright red and shiny paper hearts. Curly pink ribbons dangled from the ceiling.

Zeke saw pictures of babies with wings soaring through the sky shooting arrows.

I haven't met any human babies yet, Zeke thought. *Do they really have wings?*

Signs hung everywhere saying:

Zeke was confused. Normally, the school hallways were filled with posters and signs about school plays, sports competitions against other schools, or class projects. But this? This seemed unusual, even for humans.

Zeke stopped a boy who was hurrying to his class.

"Um, excuse me, but why is all this stuff up on the walls?" he asked.

The boy shook his head, rolled his eyes, and kept walking. Looking back over his shoulder he said, "What *planet* are you from, man?"

"Trag—" Zeke started to answer automatically, but caught himself in time. No one but his best friend Harris Walker knew that Zeke was really an alien.

Then the boy stopped and added, "Valentine's Day is next week. What else would it be?"

"I . . . don't . . . know?" Zeke replied as the boy disappeared down the hall. "And what's Valentine's Day?"

At lunchtime, Zeke sat with Harris as he usually did. He was eager to figure out what all these strange decorations were about.

"I have a question," Zeke said. "What is Valentine's Day?"

"Ah, I guess you don't have this holiday on Tragas," Harris said, being sure to keep his voice low to protect his friend's secret.

"No, we don't," Zeke admitted.

"Valentine's Day is a holiday when

you let the people that you like know that you care about them," Harris explained. "You can give them a card, some candy, a gift, or something shaped like a heart."

"Now I'm even more confused," said Zeke. "What does the organ that pumps blood through the body have to do with liking someone?"

Harris smiled. "It's just a symbol. On Earth, the heart is the place where you feel an emotion, like love. Don't you have any similar holiday like that on Tragas?"

"Well, we have Hole-tania Day," said Zeke. "That's when each being on Tragas digs a hole and fills it with pieces of furniture they no longer want. Then they invite everyone they love over to see it."

"Okay," said Harris, a little confused now himself. "Don't worry, Zeke. It's one of those things that might be easier to just experience than to explain. You'll get the hang of Valentine's Day!"

THAT AFTERNOON, THE WHOLE school gathered in the auditorium for an assembly. Zeke sat next to Harris and Roxy Martinez, who had been Harris's best friend since before kindergarten. Zeke and Roxy had become good friends, too, since Zeke's arrival on Earth.

Principal Perlman walked up to the microphone and addressed the students.

"As you all know, Valentine's Day is coming soon," she said. "But, of course, even if you didn't know that before you came to school today, that fact is hard to miss once you enter the building."

A small wave of laughter spread through the auditorium.

Zeke leaned over to Harris. "*I* missed it," he said, smiling.

Principal Perlman continued. "You all did a wonderful job decorating the school and getting us into the spirit of the holiday. And so, to further the holiday cheer and also to help your fellow students, I'm announcing a fund-raiser.

"As many of you know, the Jefferson Elementary marching band is in need of new uniforms. And so, this year for Valentine's Day, students can buy candy-grams through the school to send chocolate to a special someone. A portion of the money from each purchase will go toward the uniforms."

Principal Perlman held up a huge bar of chocolate as an example of a candy-gram.

An excited buzz of chatter spread through the room.

"This is great!" Roxy whispered to Harris. "We both love chocolate!" Zeke looked at them both, confused.

After the assembly ended, Harris, Zeke, and Roxy left the auditorium with the rest of the students.

"I still don't see what's so special about all this," Zeke said as everyone got up and headed to their next class. "Can't I buy candy from the store anytime I like?"

"It's not completely about the candy," Roxy said, "as much as I do love chocolate. It's a way to let someone know that you like them. It just doesn't have to be chocolate. It can be a card or anything heart-themed, really."

As she said this, Roxy placed her right hand over her heart.

"And buying these chocolates also helps the school," she said. "Anyway, I'm off to go get some! See you later." She hurried away.

"Actually, for someone from Tragas, our hearts are located here," Zeke said to Harris once they were alone. He took his left hand, and touched the back of his neck. "But I still don't see what any of this has to do with caring about someone."

Harris laughed. "Oh, don't worry. You'll figure it out," he said. "It will make more sense once you get a few candy-grams!"

But Zeke was not so sure.

3 A MYSTERIOUS MESSAGE

ON THE MORNING OF VALENTINE'S Day, Zeke was still as confused as ever. He worried a lot about what might happen when he got to school.

19

When he arrived, he found three giant candy bars sitting on his desk. Each one had a pink, heart-shaped card attached.

Zeke opened the first card. It was from Roxy.

He glanced over at Roxy, who smiled at Zeke.

The next Valentine was from Harris.

Zeke smiled. *Maybe Valentine's Day will be fun after all*, he thought. He looked over at Harris.

"Try the chocolate," Harris said.

Zeke unwrapped one of the chocolate bars and took a bite.

His eyes opened wide and his mouth puckered with delight. "Ohh," he moaned. "Wow! Chocolate is the best," he mumbled through a mouthful of the sweet treat.

Harris laughed at Zeke's reaction.

Zeke looked down at his third Valentine.

Hmmm . . . who could this one be from? he wondered.

Zeke opened the third card. It read:

The card had no signature, so Zeke had no idea who it was from. He felt confused, then worried. Could he have forgotten a friend who remembered him? Would he hurt someone's feelings by not figuring out who it was that liked him?

He wasn't sure what to do, so he showed the card to Harris.

"That is so great!" Harris said. "It's nice that someone else sees how awesome you are! I wonder who it is."

"But did you read what it said?" Zeke asked nervously. "'Out of this world!' There's someone else here who knows I'm really an alien!"

Harris laughed.

"No, no, Zeke," he explained. "'Out of this world' is a common Earth expression. It just means that someone thinks you're pretty terrific."

Zeke let out a big sigh and felt relieved, but he was still uneasy. Someone at school liked him, but he didn't have any clue who it was.

After school that day, Harris and Zeke were hanging out in Harris's room.

"Alright, let's use logic to try to figure out who your mystery valentine might be," Harris said.

"And how do we that?" Zeke asked.

"Well, think of the people you like," Harris said. "You know, the people you spend time with who've had a chance to get to know you a little bit since you arrived."

"Well, let's see," said Zeke, scratching his head. "There's Nancy Nash. She's on the soccer team with me. And a few weeks ago, I helped her when she got injured during a game."

"That's a good guess," said Harris. "Who else could it be?"

"Um, Debbie Darwin," Zeke said. "She's in the science club with me. We worked on a few experiments together. We seemed to get along okay."

"See? That's good thinking," said Harris. "Now we have two."

"Oh, and Jane Jeong, in my history study group," Zeke said. "We did a whole unit on ancient Egypt together. It's been difficult to learn so much unfamiliar Earth history, but she is always very friendly to me."

"Okay, then. It's got to be one of them," Harris said. "Now, we just have to figure out which one!"

THE TRAGAS TRADITIONS

THAT EVENING AT HOME, Zeke explained his problem to his parents.

"I received three chocolate bars for Valentine's Day," Zeke said.

"What is Valentine's Day?" asked Quar, his mother.

"It is a day on Earth when people let each other know that they are liked and cared about," Zeke explained. "I got a chocolate bar from Harris and one from Roxy, but I already knew that they liked me."

"They have been good friends to you," said Xad, Zeke's father. "We are very happy about that."

"Me, too," said Zeke. "But I also got a third chocolate bar from someone who did not the sign the card that comes with it. So I don't know who gave it to me or who wants to let me know that they like me."

"This Valentine's Day reminds me of Hole-tania Day back on Tragas," said Xad. "In the card, did this person invite you over to look at their discarded furniture in a hole?"

"No, it doesn't seem to work that way here," said Zeke.

"Maybe this person wants you to stack boxes until the tower is taller than themselves," suggested Quar.

As Quar said this, Xad looked into her eyes and smiled. Quar smiled back. They grasped each other's hands, started glowing, and transformed back into their true alien forms. On Earth, Quar, Xad, and Zeke took on human appearances to blend in.

When the transformation was complete, Quar and Xad both had purple skin. They each had multiple eyes. Tentacles extended from their shoulders.

"I have not thought about stacking boxes for some time now," Quar said. She wrapped one of her tentacles around Xad's body.

Zeke sighed. "I don't think Earth people know about stacking boxes," he said. "On Valentine's Day, people give each other things like gifts, paper hearts, cards, and candy."

Quar and Xad quickly reverted back into their human forms.

"Ah, and they must put these things in a hole for others to see, right?" asked Xad.

"No, I don't think so," said Zeke.

"Well, maybe they stack these things very high to show the other person they like them," suggested Quar.

"It's not like that, either," said Zeke.

"Perhaps they play a game with these cards," said Xad. "I have learned an Earth game with cards called gin rummy."

"Yes," added Quar. "And another Earth card game called hearts. Maybe that is what the paper hearts are for."

Zeke realized that his parents were not going to be much help.

"Thanks," he said, heading up to his room. "I'll figure this one out myself."

5 ON THE CASE

THE NEXT DAY AT LUNCH, Harris and Zeke tried to figure out who Zeke's mystery valentine was.

"What if you got each girl a gift?" Harris suggested. "That would show that you like them. Then, maybe whoever it is will let you know that she was the one who left the candygram!"

"I like that idea," Zeke said. "I guess I'll give it a try!"

Zeke had soccer practice the next day after school. He decided that he would give the first gift to Nancy Nash, his friend on the team. *But what should I give her?*

Sitting in his room that evening, Zeke used a piece of alien technology. He put a blinking helmet on his head and watched some Mem-Vids from his life on Tragas. The Mem-Vid helmet took actual memories from Zeke's mind and projected them on a screen as videos. As he watched, Zeke realized that as happy as he was living on Earth, there were still times that he missed Tragas.

A Mem-Vid appeared, showing a party on Tragas for his mom's birthday. Zeke watched and smiled as Xad handed Quar a bucket of squiggly, squirmy Tragas zeniworms.

"This is perfect!" Quar said in the video. "Zeniworms help keep my tentacles soft."

Zeke watched as his mother let the worms crawl all over her tentacles. She smiled with delight.

"That's it!" Zeke cried out loud. "I'll get Nancy a bucket of worms to keep her tenta . . . I mean hands, smooth. This will be the perfect Valentine's Day gift!"

The next morning before school, Zeke spent an hour in his backyard. He took a large metal bucket and filled it up with every worm he could find crawling in the grass.

This is a great idea, Zeke thought. *I'm going to give Nancy the worms after soccer practice today. If she's happy about it, then that will prove that she's the one who gave me the valentine!*

6

A SQUIRMY SITUATION

THE NEXT MORNING, ZEKE GOT to school early. He hurried to the soccer field and hid his bucket of worms behind the bleachers.

As he headed into school, Zeke began worrying.

What if Nancy is not *the one who gave me the valentine?* he thought. *Will I make a fool of myself? But she might still like the worms. After all, who wouldn't? Then again, what if she* is *the one who gave me the valentine? That means she really likes me, and I didn't even know it.*

That thought made Zeke even more nervous.

He had a hard time concentrating as he went through his morning classes. At lunch with Harris that day, he explained his plan.

"I came up with a really nice Valentine's gift," he explained. "It's something I know my mom likes a lot, so I think it will be good for Nancy."

"What is it?" Harris asked.

"I don't want to say until I see if she really likes it," said Zeke.

"Okay," said Harris. "Good luck!"

After school, Zeke hurried to soccer practice. When practice was over, he ran to the bleachers and grabbed the bucket. Holding it behind his back, he walked over to Nancy.

"Hi, Nancy," Zeke said shyly.

"Oh. Hi there, Zeke," Nancy said, smiling. "Pretty good practice, huh?"

"I need to work on my passing a bit," Zeke said.

"You'll get there," said Nancy. "It took me a while to get good. And I remember you told me that nobody played soccer at your old school."

"Uh no, we didn't," Zeke said.

Okay, stop stalling, Zeke thought. *Just give her the present.*

Zeke took a deep breath.

"So Nancy, I wanted to give you a valentine," Zeke said.

Nancy's eyes opened wide. "That is so nice of you, Zeke," she said. "Is it one of those candy-grams the school is selling?"

"No, not exactly," Zeke said. He whipped the bucket out from behind his back.

"Happy Valentine's Day, Nancy!" he shouted.

Nancy grabbed the handle, then looked down into the bucket.

"Yuck!" she shrieked, dropping the bucket and spilling the worms all over the field.

"That is so *gross,* Zeke! This isn't funny at all. Why would you think anyone would like this? This is disgusting!"

She turned and stormed away.

Huh, I guess she wasn't my valentine, after all, Zeke thought.

That evening, Zeke was hanging out with Harris. He filled him in on what happened.

Harris laughed so hard, he was almost crying. "Worms?! Really?! You gave her a bucket of worms?! What were you thinking?!"

"My mom loves worms, they make her tentacles soft," Zeke explained. "I thought Nancy might like them for the same reason. Except, of course, for her hands."

Harris shook his head, still laughing. "You should have asked me first. I would have told you that was a bad idea! Maybe Roxy can help us," Harris suggested.

The two boys quickly headed over to Roxy's house.

"A bucket of worms?" Roxy said, hearing what happened. "That is just plain weird, Zeke."

"Yes, I know that now," Zeke said.

"I think you should *make* something for the next girl," Roxy suggested. "Building something yourself that you put your own hard work into is a great way to show you care."

"Great idea!" said Harris.

"I like that idea. Thanks, Roxy!" said Zeke. "Debbie Darwin loves science projects. I'm going to make the perfect gift for her!"

THAT EVENING, ZEKE SAT IN A corner of the garage attached to his house. He stared at a pile of alien machinery that his parents had brought with them from Tragas. Xad had shown Zeke what a lot of this equipment could do, and Zeke enjoyed tinkering with it.

Time to get busy, Zeke thought.

He lined up a bunch of circuits, dials, and knobs on a workbench. Using some of the Tragas tools, Zeke constructed a metal frame in the shape of a box. He then took a sheet of Trass—super-thin Tragas glass—and made panels on all sides of the box.

Zeke began setting up a complicated contraption. Using his alien power of moving objects with his mind, he moved a series of arms, levers, and steel balls into the box.

Xad stepped into the garage.

"What's that supposed to be?" he asked.

"It's a cosmic clock," Zeke explained. "As the arms rotate, they drop these little steel balls into grooved wooden tracks that spin around. When the balls stop moving, they land in these holes.

"Using this, you can not only tell what time it is on Earth, but also on any other planet in this solar system. And you can also predict when there is going to be an eclipse or shooting stars."

"Very well done, Zeke," said Xad.

"Right now I'm just making it move using my mind abilities," Zeke explained. "What I need to find now is a power source."

Xad pressed his fingers on either sides of his head. Using his own mind powers, he made a large silver box float down from a high shelf. Zeke looked into the box and saw what looked like a bunch of glowing purple buttons.

"Wow!" said Zeke. "What are those?"

"Barzium crystals," Xad explained. "They are mined on Tragas. These crystals can provide power to big machines. One should be more than enough to power your cosmic clock."

Zeke stopped using his powers and the cosmic clock stopped moving. Then he slipped one of the Barzium crystals into the clock. The arms started rotating again, and the steel balls spun around the track.

"Thanks, Xad!" Zeke said. "This is going to be a perfect Valentine's gift. And Debbie will never have to change its batteries!"

The next day after school, the science club met. Zeke hid his cosmic clock in the back of the room.

Zeke and Debbie Darwin worked together on an experiment during the club meeting. As always, they got along really well.

I think she likes me, thought Zeke. *She's going to love the cosmic clock!*

After the science club meeting, Zeke grabbed her gift and handed it to Debbie.

"Happy Valentine's Day, Debbie," Zeke said. "I made this for you."

"Um, thanks," said Debbie, looking both surprised and confused. "So . . . what is it?"

"It's a cosmic clock," Zeke explained. "Watch!"

Zeke pressed the Barzium crystal, and the inside of the clock started to move. He was thrilled to see Debbie's eyes light up as the arms and balls spun through the contraption.

"Wow, Zeke, this must have taken an awful lot of work," said Debbie. "This is so nice of you!"

Then suddenly, everything started moving faster and faster. The arms spun wildly, sending the steel balls crashing through the Trass. They bounced all over the floor. Then one of the arms flew off and hit Debbie's head.

"Ow! Is this some kind of weird prank?" she asked, and she ran out of the room.

The Barzium crystal must have been too strong for such a small machine! Zeke thought. *Now I'm never going to find out who sent me that valentine. And even worse, I'm losing friends every day!*

THE NEXT DAY ON THE BUS RIDE to school, Zeke told Roxy and Harris about what happened with Debbie.

"Sounds like you tried to do something nice," Roxy said, hoping to comfort her friend. "Building something from scratch that you designed yourself says a lot about how much you care for the person you give it to."

"Yeah, too bad it blew up," added Harris.

Roxy glared at Harris.

"What? It did!" said Harris.

"I think I'm just going to give up on Valentine's Day and trying to figure out who sent me that chocolate," Zeke said as the three friends reached school. "I'd probably mess things up even if I knew who it was."

"No, you wouldn't," said Roxy. "Any kid would be lucky to have you for a friend."

"Yeah," added Harris. "Just look at us! We're both happy you're our friend."

Zeke nodded, but remained quiet the rest of the way as they walked into school.

At recess that day, Zeke sat by himself in the playground, feeling sad. And, for the first time since he became friends with Roxy and Harris, Zeke felt homesick.

As kids ran and played all around him, Zeke thought about his life back on Tragas.

I always knew what was what on Tragas, he thought. *I knew what all the holidays were and how I was supposed to celebrate them. I knew the customs and I didn't feel embarrassed by not knowing what the right thing to do was.*

And, for the first time in a long time, Zeke thought about going home. *Maybe it's time to go back to a life we know. Maybe my parents' research on Earth will end soon and we can all go home.*

"Are you okay, Zeke?" asked a familiar girl's voice. "You look kind of sad sitting here all by yourself."

Zeke felt a little embarrassed that someone had caught him siting there feeling sorry for himself. He didn't even look up.

"Someone gave me a valentine," he explained.

"That doesn't sound like a reason to be sad," said the girl.

"Well, whoever it was didn't sign the card," Zeke said. "I have no idea who it was. I took a couple of guesses, but when I tried to give gifts to the girls I thought it might be, everything went wrong. They both hated the gifts."

"Well, maybe neither of those girls was the one who gave you the valentine," said the girl. "Maybe your true valentine would like whatever you gave her because she likes *you*."

"Hmm . . ." Zeke groaned, thinking about what the girl has just said.

"Now, if *I* was going to get something from *my* valentine, I would like to get a poem," said the girl.

Zeke looked up and saw Jane Jeong, the girl from his history study group— the third girl Zeke had suspected of giving him the valentine!

"WHA—IT'S YOU!" ZEKE CRIED. "*You* gave me the valentine!" He wasn't sure if he was happy, nervous, or both.

"I did," said Jane, turning to leave. She turned back to Zeke. "And I like poems." Then she blushed a little and ran away.

Zeke was stunned. *I have to tell Harris and Roxy about this!*

That evening, Zeke was at Harris's house, hanging out with Harris and Roxy. He told them the whole story.

"Sometimes when you have a problem, the solution comes along when you least expect it," said Roxy.

"Sounds to me like you better get busy writing a poem," said Harris.

Zeke's face grew serious.

"I've never written a poem before," he said. "How do I even start?"

"Just start writing down ideas, thoughts, and images, especially ones that make you think of Jane," said Roxy. "You can work on rhyming things after you have some basic ideas."

"Okay," said Zeke. "I'm going to go home and try. See you guys tomorrow."

At home, Zeke got to work. Using his power of mind-projection, Zeke pressed his fingertips against the sides of his head. A large screen appeared just above him. As he thought of things he wanted to write, the words appeared on the big screen.

Let's see what I can say about Jane, Zeke thought. *I like her hair. It's black, like the cheese is on Tragas. Oh, that's good!*

Zeke started his poem: "The color of your hair reminds me of cheese. I like the way it blows in the breeze."

I like that. What else?

How about: "I think you're very nice, just like friendly Tragonian mice."

Or: "A Kraka beast you could disarm, with just your smile, your laugh, your charm. Being with you is so much fun, even if I lost at Bonkas, I'd think I'd won."

This isn't so hard! Still, I think I should show it to Harris before I give it to Jane.

The next day, Zeke went to Harris's house and showed him the poem.

"Um, I like the way you rhyme things," Harris said. "But while all this may make sense on Tragas, Jane's not really going to understand a lot of it."

"Huh? What do you mean, Harris?" asked Zeke.

"Well, saying that her hair is the color of cheese may be a compliment on Tragas, since the cheese there is black. But on Earth, cheese that's black is likely moldy and rotten, so she might not take that too well."

"Oh, good point," said Zeke.

"Also, what are Tragonian mice?" Harris asked.

"They are big mice on Tragas," Zeke explained. "Some are as big as dogs. They are very friendly . . . like Jane."

"Yeah, but mice tend to freak people out here on Earth," Harris explained. "The thought of a mouse as big as a dog is pretty scary, even to me. And I'm pretty sure she's not going to know what a Kraka beast or Bonkas is."

"Hmm . . . I think I get what you're saying," said Zeke. "I'd better get busy rewriting. I want to give Jane the poem tomorrow!"

ZEKE STAYED UP LATE THAT NIGHT working and reworking his poem. Finally, when he was happy with what he had written, he went to bed.

The next day, all he could think about was giving the poem to Jane. When classes finally ended, Zeke hurried to his history study group that was about to start.

He peeked into the room.

Good! he thought. *Jane isn't here yet.*

Zeke snuck over to where Jane usually sat and left a pink envelope covered in red hearts on Jane's desk. Inside the envelope was his poem.

A few minutes later, Jane came into the room. When she reached her desk, she smiled. Opening the colorful envelope, she read the poem to herself:

I like the way you smile.
I like your kind of style.
I like the things you do,
but mostly, I like you.
You're always nice to me.
You always help me see
that friends mean lots to you.
They mean that to me, too.
So here's a thought for you.
I hope you like it, too.
Thanks for being a friend of mine.
Jane, please be my valentine!

Jane finished reading the poem. She put down the paper and smiled warmly at Zeke. "Thank you, Zeke," she said. "I love this. It's really beautiful. And I can't think of a better valentine's gift."

"I'm glad you like it," said Zeke.
"Would you like to walk home together after study group?" she asked.
"Sure!" said Zeke, smiling.

When the history study group ended, Zeke and Jane walked from the school together.

"So, tell me the name again of the place you're from," Jane said.

"It's called Tragas," Zeke said. "My parents and I moved here not long ago. They are researchers, and so they travel a lot. Because of that, I've lived in a bunch of different places."

"What's Tragas like?" Jane asked.

"In some ways, it's not that different than Ea—than here," Zeke said, almost slipping and saying "Earth."

"Kids go to school, play games, the usual stuff," Zeke added. "Some of the trees and lakes and mountains look quite different though."

"Sounds beautiful," said Jane. "Maybe I'll get to see it someday."

"Yeah, maybe," laughed Zeke, not sure how that would ever happen.

A few minutes later, they reached Jane's house.

"Thanks again for the wonderful poem, Zeke, and Happy Valentine's Day!" Jane said. Then she gave Zeke a hug and ran into her house.

Zeke walked the rest of the way home feeling great. Any thoughts about going back to Tragas left his mind. *It still might take me a while to figure out how things work on Earth, but I'm glad to be living here.*

When Zeke got home, Harris and Roxy were waiting for him in front of his house.

"So, how did it go?" Roxy asked.
"Great!" said Zeke.

He filled them in about how much Jane liked his poem. Then he reached into his bag and pulled out a chocolate bar for Roxy and another one for Harris.

"Happy Valentine's Day!" Zeke said.

"Awesome! Thanks, Zeke! I'm glad you finally understand how much fun Valentine's Day can be," said Harris.

"Yes, and I'm glad both of you are my friends!" Zeke said.

Then the three friends went into Zeke's house to play some video games and eat their chocolate bars.

Read on for a sneak peek at the seventh book in the Alien Next Door series!

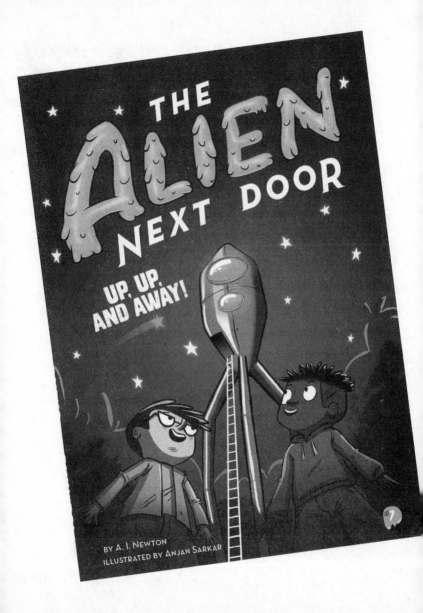

THE ALIEN NEXT DOOR

UP, UP, AND AWAY!

BY A. I. NEWTON
ILLUSTRATED BY ANJAN SARKAR

1

HOME, AT LAST

HARRIS WALKER AND HIS FRIEND
Zeke were walking home from school.
They were both in great moods.

"Spring break!" Harris shouted. "A
whole week off from school! We can
hang out and do whatever we want!"

"And this happens the same time
every year?" asked Zeke.

"Pretty much," replied Harris.

"Hmm . . ." said Zeke. "Back home
on Tragas, breaks only happen after

we learn how to do something really well. Then we spend the whole break in meditation pods reviewing all we've learned up to that point."

Harris smiled. Zeke had very quickly become one of his best friends. He still found it amazing that Zeke was from another planet.

"That sounds okay, I guess. Since you're probably learning how to move things with your mind!" Harris said. "But is it as much fun as the time we went camping?"

"I have to admit, I didn't understand at first why anyone would want to sleep outside," Zeke said. "But once we did it, I did have fun."

"And I'll never forget the look on your face when you first saw a waterfall here," Harris said.

Zeke smiled. "I could not believe that the water flowed down from the top," he said. "On Tragas, waterfalls flow up!"

"Now *that*, I'd like to see!" said Harris.

"You never know," said Zeke. "Maybe some day, you'll get to visit Tragas."

"I don't know if I could survive eating only Tragas food," said Harris. "Remember the first time my parents saw food from your planet?"

"I sure do," said Zeke. "They were

polite to my parents, but I could see that they were a little freaked out."

"I was, too!" said Harris. "When I saw those slimy orange slugs your folks brought . . ."

"Kreslars," Zeke said. "They are the most popular food on Tragas."

"Yeah, well, I wouldn't open a Kreslar stand on Earth," Harris joked. "I don't think you'd sell very many."

Zeke laughed. "I guess, but there are a lot of things about Earth that I still don't completely get. Like Halloween and Valentine's Day. They both turned out to be fun, but I still think they are kind of weird."

The boys arrived at their houses,

which were next door to each other.

"Come over and hang out after dinner?" Harris asked as he opened the front door to his house.

"Sure," said Zeke. "See you later."

As he walked across his front lawn, Zeke thought about how, after a hard beginning, he really was enjoying his time here on Earth. Then he stepped through his front door.

Zeke was shocked to see his parents packing things into boxes.

"What's going on?" he asked.

"Guess what, Zeke?" said Xad, his father. "We're going home . . . to Tragas!"

Journey to some magical places, rock out, and find your inner superhero with these other chapter book series from **Little Bee Books!**